MW00982341

12.95

Playing Bare

Dominic Champagne

translated by
Shelley Tepperman

Talonbooks Vancouver 1993

Published with the assistance of the Canada Council

Talonbooks
201-1019 East Cordova St.
Vancouver, B.C.
Canada V6A 1M8

Typeset in New Baskerville by Pièce de Résistance Ltée., and printed and bound in Canada by Hignell Printing Ltd.

First printing: October 1993

Playing Bare was first published by VLB Éditeur, Montreal, Quebec.

Canadian Cataloguing in Publication Data

Champagne, Dominic, 1963—

[La Répétition. English]
Playing bare

A play.
Translation of: La répétition.
ISBN 0-88922-335-1

I. Title. II. Title: Répétition. English.
PS8555.H346R413 1993   C842'.54   C93-091777-4
PQ3919.2.C493R413 1993

From *La Répétition* to *Playing Bare*

Playing Bare, the English translation of *La Répétition*, was commissioned by Street People Theatre and developed in collaboration with various organizations. An early version of the translation titled *The Rehearsal*, was workshopped in 1991 in conjunction with Ruby Slippers Productions at the Vancouver Fringe Festival. In December of that year, the script received a translation workshop and Freefall staged reading at Playwrights' Workshop Montreal. The final version was completed with the assistance of the Carnegie Mellon Showcase for New Plays. Street People Theatre presented the premiere production at Montreal's Théâtre La Chapelle during the festival Les 20 jours du théâtre à risque in November of 1992; the production then had a full run at La Chapelle from February 12 to March 7, 1993.

Street People Theatre's premiere production was directed by Katrina Dunn with the set and lighting by Louis Beaudoin and costumes by Karin Jones. The Stage Manager was Rebecca Miller; Shelley Tepperman was Assistant Director. The cast was as follows:

BLANCHE...Lynne Adams
LUCE ....Paulina Abarca
ETIENNE ....Bruce Dinsmore
VICTOR..Chris Heyerdahl
PIPPA* ....Sheena Larkin
PIANIST ....Nicholas Pynes

*In this production, Pipo was played as a woman, with minor changes to the text.

La Répétition was first produced by the Théâtre Il Va Sans Dire at the Salle Fred Barry from January 8 to February 3, 1990. Dominic Champagne directed the following cast:

BLANCHE...Julie Castonguay
LUCE ....Sylvie Drapeau
ETIENNE...Luc Gouin
VICTOR..Norman Helms
PIPO..Marc Legault
PIANIST ....Christian Thomas

Key collaborators included the following:

Assistant Director/Stage Manager ....André Barnard
Set ....Jean Bard
Stage Fresco ....Pascale Poulin
Costumes ....Francois Saint-Aubin
Lighting ....Lou Arteau
Original Music ....Christian Thomas
Technical Direction ....Guy Lemire

The original French text was published in 1990 by VLB Éditeur in Montreal. It was shortlisted for the 1991 Governor General's Award for French drama.

Translator's Acknowledgments:

Many people contributed to the development of this translation. Thanks to Michael Devine and Frank Gagliano, Artistic Directors of Playwrights' Workshop Montreal and the Carnegie Mellon Showcase of New Plays respectively, for their support of the project. The Canada Council Writing and Publication Section provided a much appreciated translation grant. I am grateful to colleagues and friends who read different versions of the translation and made valuable comments: Garry Bowers, Elyse Buchbinder, Douglas Cooper, Katrina Dunn, Norman Helms, Alan Nashman, Robert Nunn, and Denise Parent. The intelligence and imagination of the actors and directors who participated in the various workshops and readings did much to refine playability and strengthen the characters' voices. Special thanks to Diane Brown, Florentia Conway, Katrina Dunn, Nona Gerard, Randall Haynes, Pam Howard-Jones, David Francis, Mladen Kiselov, Shannon Lawson, Pierre Lenoir, Michael Mawson, Paul Miller, Elizabeth Orion, Joseph Shaw, Aron Tager, and Don Wadsworth: You have all left your marks in or between the lines. Maureen Labonté was a stimulating and insightful dramaturg, and as Artistic Director of Street People Theatre, Paulina Abarca was a source of astute feedback at every stage and was committed to seeing this script brought to life in English. Finally, thanks to Dominic Champagne, responsible for the initial spark and enduring inspiration, for his faultless ear, his generosity, and his "grande disponibilité."

Note: This translation incorporates revisions made by the author subsequent to the French-language publication. Significant changes have been made to Scenes 7 and 8 in particular.

Set and Staging

When the audience enters the pianist is already seated downstage right, playing a gentle, inviting overture that shifts between slow blues and an uptempo fugue. On the piano are a bottle of scotch and a half-filled glass, an ashtray, and a pack of cigarettes.

Towards stage left, upstage from the piano, are a table and four chairs. On the table are a small standing mirror, sticks of greasepaint, jars of powder, a sewing machine, a copy of Beckett's *Waiting for Godot*, a reel-to-reel tape recorder, and some paper. Also on the table are the props for a performance of *Godot*: four dusty, black bowler hats, a long rope, a whip, a pipe and a pouch of tobacco, a wine bottle filled with water, etc. (These objects could also be in the wings until Blanche brings them onstage in the course of the play.)

Upstage left is something like a tree. Farther upstage, on the stage left wall, is a door leading to Blanche's storage room. On the same wall downstage from this door is another door leading to Pipo's office. Upstage, near the storage room door, stands a ladder reaching the ceiling.

All elements of the set, stage management, lighting, costumes, and props are visible to the audience. The setting should feel like the backstage of a theatre set. The walls are the real theatre walls, painted as black as possible. They may be covered with pipes, electrical cables, flies, rigging, fastened curtains, etc. A shadowy fresco is barely visible on the back wall: a subtle encounter of bodies tearing at each other.

The lighting is at times bright and full, at other times (the bar scenes) low and intimate, designed to accentuate the physical presence of the actors. The effect is hazy, unsettling, as though everything is floating.

The costumes should heighten the strange, clownish, dreamlike, ritual presence of the actors performing that night. The colour black dominates, providing a certain unity in set and costumes.

The makeup, without seeming "mask-like," should make it obvious that we are watching a performance, that the actors are made up to play something. Very pale faces, perhaps.

The music should be at times light and bouncy (inspired by Bach suites and fugues, or ragtime, for example) and at times heavy and languorous. For the bar scenes, gutsy jazz or vintage Southern blues.

We should generally expect warmth: the first requirement of the aesthetic should be a subtle humanity.

When the pianist segues from Gershwin's "Summertime" into a kind of funeral march, the play has begun.

The "fugue":

The fugue (heard especially at the beginning of the scenes) serves as ETIENNE and VICTOR's signature music. Towards the end of the play it becomes slower and darker, without, however, spilling into pathos.

The "beats":

The expression "a beat" is used throughout the script to indicate moments where the passing of time may be accented by a musical device. In the original production a repeated piano note was used.

ETIENNE's noises:

"Hnnhh" denotes a kind of reverse sniff, the sound of air exhaled pointedly through the nostrils. These sounds mark ETIENNE's non- verbal but significant reactions to LUCE. The actor playing ETIENNE is welcome to substitute another type of sound or a gesture.

Errare humanum est

I would like to dedicate this play to each of the 25,000 people who will not be at this theatre this evening, or tomorrow, or ever. To each one of these 25,000 wanderers of my city, who have left everything behind them—their families, their talents, their well-being—and who seek, without finding. I hope I have captured something of their pain in this humble work.

I would also like to dedicate this play to my son Jules, and to my friend André Barnard, and to the six magnificent actors who will bring this play to life this evening, and tomorrow, and again and again—six princes of the realm of the ephemeral who have given up their lives, their talent, and their souls, and who seek, and who have sought with me for months. There is much of their greatness in this small work.

Finally, I would like to wish you, the audience, an entertaining evening, because, as Pascal said, a king without entertainment is a man of sorrows, and it's always better when you don't think too much about it!

...it was never stories, any old thing, the same old thing, for as long as you can remember, no, longer than that, any old thing, the same old thing, to pass the time, then, as time didn't pass, for no reason at all, in your thirst, trying to cease and never ceasing, seeking the cause, the cause of talking...

—Samuel Beckett, *The Unnamable*

"Dada"
—Jules' first word

Scene 1

Funeral march.

Shadowy half-light.

LUCE enters, a bouquet of withered flowers in her arms. She stops centre stage and kneels in silence.

LUCE   "All living things, so many lives; all living things, having completed their mournful cycle, have been snuffed out. Centuries have passed, a century of centuries. The earth is lonely for life, and the poor moon now casts its glow in vain. No longer do the cranes waken with a cry in the meadow; and in the linden groves the hum of beetles is no longer heard. It is cold. It is cold inside the cold. I am empty. I am emptier than empty. All is dreadful. More frightening than dreadful. All is deserted. I am alone. Alone."[1]

Noise from the wings.

The stage work lights come on.

BLANCHE   *Off* Come on!

BLANCHE enters, a lighting pole in hand.

BLANCHE   It's over now. It's been over for more than an hour. You were fabulous but it's over. Can it.

LUCE   I was off from beginning to end. My whole existence is an open wound. An open wound full of pus.

---

[1] Anton Chekhov, *The Seagull*, translator's adaptation.

11

BLANCHE	Is that right. Come on, Luce.
LUCE	I have nothing left to give them. I feel like a student who's just racked up her fifth Ph.D. and still doesn't know where she's going.
BLANCHE	*Picking up the flowers* You've had standing ovations thirty nights straight. We could have kept running all winter if you'd wanted.
LUCE	I can't go on, Blanche. I'm empty.
BLANCHE	It's Nina who just died, not you.
LUCE	Listen! Listen to the theatre! Do you hear that? That's the last piece of my soul flying away with her.
BLANCHE	No it's not! There are pigeons caught in the rafters. We could hear them when you were onstage. I'll take care of it tomorrow.
LUCE	Listen! The last lines have flown away; the lights are out. The applause dies down. The theatre empties out. And...the great actress is all alone with herself once again.
BLANCHE & LUCE	Her nose buried in the opening night flowers already withered...
BLANCHE	...full of dust and cobwebs. I know.
LUCE	This silence is going to swallow me up.
BLANCHE	Boy, I thank the good Lord for not making *me* a slave to *my* emotions.

LUCE	I can't stand it anymore.
BLANCHE	It's over now. Come, take off your make-up.
LUCE	No, I don't feel like it.
BLANCHE	Come on.

Melancholy piano.

LUCE advances slowly towards the table, frightened by the sight of the mirror. Her face convulses grotesquely.

BLANCHE gives her a pill.

BLANCHE	Here, take your pill, it'll calm you down.

LUCE swallows the pill.

Silence.

LUCE	*Looking at herself in the mirror* Shit!
BLANCHE	Don't look at yourself, you know you can't stand it. Do you ever see me looking in the mirror?
LUCE	Farewell, Nina...
BLANCHE	Hey, come on. Let yourself live a little.
LUCE	What's living?
BLANCHE	Here. Take this. At least take off the worst of it, OK?

She drops a towel on LUCE's head.

LUCE	Didn't have time to learn how to live. My lucky star...shit on my head too early.
BLANCHE	Oh Lord!
LUCE	Tiny Talent Time ruined my future when I was ten.
BLANCHE	Listen to her! Every actress in town would give anything to be in her shoes.
LUCE	Go on, act! Play after play after play. Act! Don't stop acting!

BLANCHE sighs impatiently.

LUCE	I'm watching my life from the wings, Blanche!
BLANCHE	Luce, you have to take your make-up off or else you'll make a fool of yourself again when you leave.
LUCE	*Pointing to her reflection* I don't want to see that.
BLANCHE	The sooner you come back to earth, the sooner you can go and get drunk, the sooner you'll have forgotten that it's you there.
LUCE	But the bar will end up emptying out too, just like the theatre.
BLANCHE	I promise I'll stay with you until you're asleep.

LUCE	What's the point of getting sober if you just have to get drunk again?
BLANCHE	OK. Here. Put these on and get yourself together. We're getting out of here.

BLANCHE hands LUCE a pair of dark glasses and exits into the wings.

LUCE	*Putting her glasses on* Do I look all right? Do I look all right?

Melancholy piano.

LUCE	Talk to me.

The theatre lights go out.

BLANCHE returns, nose buried in her notebook. She bustles about.

BLANCHE	With or without the glasses?
LUCE	You always said you would never feel sorry for me.
BLANCHE	I said that? When?
LUCE	Blanche!
BLANCHE	You've never looked so...despairing.
LUCE	More, or less than Nina?
BLANCHE	There's no comparison.
LUCE	More than Antigone?

BLANCHE	Antigone wasn't desperate. She knew where she was going.
LUCE	Ophelia?
BLANCHE	Carol Burnett. You look like Carol Burnett in the cleaning lady sketch. All that's missing is the mop and pail. You satisfied?
LUCE	I'm losing it, Blanche, I'm going to pieces.
BLANCHE	Maybe if you didn't always wear black your thoughts wouldn't be so gloomy.
LUCE	I'm in mourning for all those who are dead inside of me. All those who have torn away a piece of my soul and flown away with it. "So many lives," Blanche, "so many lives have been snuffed out..."
BLANCHE	OK, OK, let's look ahead and move on to something else, all right?
LUCE	Sure. But to what? I'm empty.
BLANCHE	It won't go to waste. One day you might have to play a character who's completely empty and you'll be glad to have gone through this.
LUCE	I can't go on like this.
BLANCHE	Come on! In a few days you'll find another role, and it'll fill you up and you'll come back to life.

LUCE	And then the character will die, and I'll have to face myself, and I'll start drinking again. I can't keep going like this. I don't know who I am anymore.
BLANCHE	This is masochism, Luce.
LUCE	No, it's anthropology.
BLANCHE	Are you finished?
LUCE	You can feel the despair though, can't you?
BLANCHE	Yes, but it seems to me there's a slight lack of soul.
LUCE	I lack soul?
BLANCHE	Let's go, Luce.
LUCE	Leave. Leave me. Leave me alone.
BLANCHE	Oh Lord.

A beat.

BLANCHE leaves.

Piano bar.

LUCE	Ha! I lack soul, eh? I lack soul? Ooh! I lack soul! Awwww.

All right. All right!

The PIANIST stops.

Play, keep on playing.

Scene 2

Fugue.

VICTOR and ETIENNE enter through the audience from opposite sides. VICTOR walks with stiff little steps. ETIENNE limps, supporting himself with a cane.

VICTOR   Once upon a time there were two childhood friends.

ETIENNE   Etienne...

VICTOR   And Victor...who ambled through life, each in his own way, Victor on his two-wheeled bike...

ETIENNE   And Etienne in his four-wheeled rustmobile.

VICTOR   One fine morning when it was raining cats and dogs, Victor was pedalling cheerfully along, reading his newspaper, when... when...

ETIENNE   When out of the blue, Etienne's rustmobile, which was clunking along in her own sweet way, encountered Victor's bike.

VICTOR   That's right! By an extraordinary twist of fate, *that* morning Victor's bike ended up underneath Etienne's rustmobile while Victor's face ended up on the..., on the...

ETIENNE   Windshield.

VICTOR   That's it, his nose stuck in a wiper that kept

on wiping 'cause it was pouring that particular morning.

ETIENNE   But that's not the important part.

VICTOR   Oh no?

ETIENNE   No.

VICTOR   That's true, what was important, at that moment, was Victor's joy.

ETIENNE   No, it was Etienne's astonishment. Etienne's astonishment because, as the wipers cleared away the blood on the windshield, Etienne not only recognized the childhood friend he hadn't seen for quite some time, but he saw him smile from ear to ear.

VICTOR   To better understand Victor's smile, Etienne would have had to look at the other windshield wiper...

ETIENNE   Not the one that Victor's nose was stuck in, the other one.

VICTOR   Where Victor's hand was swishing back and forth, holding a scrap of paper that he had managed to save from his newspaper at the moment of impact, and on which the illiterate Etienne would have been able to read:

ETIENNE   "Theatre desperately seeking two childhood friends to live profound existential drama. No actors please."

VICTOR   So, it was due to this extraordinary twist of

19

fate that Victor was going to drag his child-hood friend Etienne into his adventure.

They go over to the tree and stop there.

A beat.

Nothing happens.

BLANCHE enters, clipboard in hand.

BLANCHE   All right, while we're waiting for her to arrive let's have a look at your resumés. If you don't have the life experience of these characters, there's no point having you wait for nothing.

VICTOR   Oh it's no problem. We have all the time in the world. Etienne, give the lady your resumé.

ETIENNE   My what?

VICTOR   Really, Etienne.

BLANCHE   You don't have a resumé?

ETIENNE   Whaddya want me to do with one of those?

VICTOR   Etienne, really!

BLANCHE moves to the table.

VICTOR   A resumé is the first step to achieving your career objective.

ETIENNE   Whadda you know about it?

VICTOR	Anyway, on my resumé I, uh, the photograph, uh, I know it's a bit on the flattering side, but it is me.
BLANCHE	Oh yes?
VICTOR	Yes yes.
BLANCHE	I think she'll prefer the real you.
VICTOR	Oh, really? Well, thank you. That's the first time anyone's told me that.

A beat.

Nothing happens.

ETIENNE	Whadda we do now?
VICTOR	We wait, Etienne, we wait.

LUCE enters.

LUCE	I'm sorry I'm late. For the last hour I've been waiting outside the door wondering how to make my entrance, and nothing "dropped in."
VICTOR	Oh really?
ETIENNE	Hnnhh.
LUCE	Give me my pill please, my head is going to burst.
BLANCHE	Oh Lord! What time did you go to bed?

LUCE	Don't give me a hard time, I've got this hammering at the base of my skull and it's sending shock waves right down to my sacrum.
BLANCHE	Did you drink a large glass of water before going to bed?
LUCE	I haven't had water at home for three days. The plumbing is shot!

> *BLANCHE gives LUCE a pill. She swallows it.*

BLANCHE	All right. These are the last. They're all I could find that seemed to fit the bill. The one with the limp is Etienne, for Estragon, and the other one is...
VICTOR	I'm Victor.
BLANCHE	Victor, right.
LUCE	Etienne.
VICTOR	Sorry.
LUCE	Come here, please.

> *A beat.*

> *Nothing happens.*

VICTOR	Well, go on.

> *ETIENNE advances, limping.*

LUCE	Your feet are causing you pain, huh?

ETIENNE	Ya, so?
LUCE	What kind of pain?
ETIENNE	You name it.
BLANCHE	Looks to me like he's got flat feet.
ETIENNE	Uh huh.
LUCE	Any corns?
ETIENNE	Lots.
LUCE	Bunions?
ETIENNE	One on each foot, ya.
LUCE	Athlete's foot?
ETIENNE	This got somethin' ta do with the part?
LUCE	Would you be the type to suffer in silence?
ETIENNE	Whinin's for wimps.
LUCE	I understand, yes. There are times in one's life when it's not easy to expose oneself. But you, Etienne, *you* have the advantage of having lived. You've *lived*, Etienne, haven't you?
ETIENNE	Ya. So?
LUCE	If we want to become friends, it's important for me that your feet hurt. I need them to.

ETIENNE	Uh hunh.
LUCE	In *Godot*, Estragon spends half the play sitting because his feet hurt so much from having walked from one place to another all his life. Do you understand?
ETIENNE	Do I ever.
BLANCHE	So, do you get athlete's foot, yes or no?
ETIENNE	Ya.
LUCE	Do you have an ingrown toenail?
ETIENNE	Two of 'em. And I got planter's warts too. An' I broke both heels seven years ago fallin' offa table in a club up north. So these two feet o' mine're good for just about nuthin' 'cept the garbage, is that what you're after?
BLANCHE	I'm sure she wasn't asking for that much.
ETIENNE	Ya well, I wasn't askin' for that much neither.
LUCE	You fell off a table?
ETIENNE	Ya.
LUCE	In a club?
ETIENNE	I was a gogoboy by profession. But it made me wanna puke to see people eyein' my cock seven nights a week. And so one night I threw myself to the ground.

LUCE	Good Heavens!
BLANCHE	How do you spell "gogoboy"?
ETIENNE	Oh boy, I dunno.
LUCE	Does the role interest you?
ETIENNE	Only thing I know how to do in life is be on a stage. Might as well try out this acting business.
VICTOR	Really, Etienne.
ETIENNE	Anyways, between this and somethin' else, I like this OK and I ain't got nothin' else.
VICTOR	Etienne, really.
BLANCHE	She's asking if the part interests you.
ETIENNE	Didn't I answer?
LUCE	Have you read the play?
ETIENNE	Yeah. I didn't understand a thing.
LUCE	I thank you, Etienne. It's comforting to have you here. Your squarish build, your lovely virile modesty, your faintly brutish side. Yes, it's comforting to see how alive you are. You already excite me. I hope we'll be able to become friends.
ETIENNE	Uh, we'll see.
LUCE	Yes...

BLANCHE	Victor.
VICTOR	Yes?
BLANCHE	Will you come here.

A beat.

Nothing happens.

VICTOR	Etienne.

He indicates to ETIENNE to come and take his place.

ETIENNE returns to the tree. VICTOR advances.

VICTOR	Hello. Before we begin I'd just like to say that I have a lot of admiration for you. I like your work very much. It really speaks to me. I think you're the best actress of your generation. And I'm not the one who said it.
LUCE	Who did?
VICTOR	Huh?
LUCE	Who said it?
VICTOR	Uh... well...
BLANCHE	Wait a minute. Didn't the ad say no actors?
VICTOR	Yes, yes, but...
LUCE	Have you ever done any acting, Victor?

VICTOR	Well...yes. Uh... Its just that... No, not really. It's not for lack of talent, it's just that my lucky star is in its hidden phase, I think.
LUCE	I want things to be *transparent* between us, Victor. Have you acted before?
VICTOR	Well, its just that in my career path since I left university, uh, I...
BLANCHE	Have you ever acted, yes or no?
VICTOR	I've only done a couple of bit parts.
LUCE	Shit.
VICTOR	But I never had more than one line. And I'm not trying to brag, but the last time my scene ended up on the cutting room floor. OK, they left my name in the credits but you can't really count that, can you?
LUCE	Well...it's sounding better.
VICTOR	I thank you.
LUCE	Do you have a venereal disease at present?
	Pause
VICTOR	In what sense?
LUCE	Transparent, Victor, *limpid.*
VICTOR	That's part of the requirements, huh?
BLANCHE	Do you have one, yes or no?

VICTOR	Well, it's just that, I had a bout of gono...gonorrhea but well, it's just cleared up.
LUCE	Shit.
VICTOR	But then again I'm sure something else is starting up. I couldn't tell you what just yet, but I'm sure I have another one. OK?
BLANCHE	You'll go and get tested when you leave.
VICTOR	That's exactly what I was thinking of doing. Will that make you happy?
LUCE	I would ask you not to utter that word in my presence, if you please.
VICTOR	Pardon me, it wasn't intentional.
LUCE	The word "happy" is so trite nowadays. Happiness. It doesn't mean anything anymore, the word "happiness." It's like the word "sadness." Today no one ever says they're sad. In another era, before Hiroshima, people still said it. But today people aren't "sad" anymore. They're tired. They aren't unhappy, they're sick. As if they had nothing left but their bodies to show us their souls. Did I take my pill, Blanche?
BLANCHE	Yes yes.
LUCE	Thank you. Where was I?
BLANCHE	Victor's suffering.

VICTOR	My suffering, yes.
LUCE	Oh yes... Do you suffer from anything else that might be relevant to the character of Vladimir?
VICTOR	You mean like, down there? Well, I have trouble going to the bathroom...sitting down.
BLANCHE	And do you go "standing up"?
VICTOR	A lot. Much too much. And on top of that, I have kidney stones.
LUCE	My God.
VICTOR	And I wouldn't want to sound like I'm laying it on, but *there's* a disease that really makes a person sad, yes yes, I mean psychologically, but it comes out physically too, in the sense that it brings on all kinds of little ailments, like psoriasis, when I'm having a hard time, like being made fun of or rejected, or feeling all alone or...
BLANCHE	How do you spell psoriasis?
VICTOR	*Quickly* P-s-o-r-i-a-s-y-s... Or s-i-s. No, I think it's a "y." We're never sure of anything in life, huh?
LUCE	No... This morning on my way to the theatre, I didn't even know if I was coming here to act or if I was coming here to act.
VICTOR	Really?

ETIENNE	Huh?

A beat.

Nothing happens.

VICTOR	*Panicking* Uh... Maybe you think that I don't have the life experience to play a sixty-year-old, but let me tell you that there are people who at thirty are already ancient, as though they had done their whole life's suffering before their time.
LUCE	How old are you?
VICTOR	I was born on a Good Friday, around 3 p.m., exactly thirty years ago.
LUCE	Yes... Yes... I too was thirty once. We all end up being thirty, one day or another, hmm? Those of us who make it that far, in any case.
VICTOR	That's for sure.

A beat.

Nothing happens.

LUCE	Thank you, that will be all.
VICTOR	It's over then? But... Do we seem like we'll do?
BLANCHE	We'll call you. Thank you.
VICTOR	She's not sure about us, is that it?

BLANCHE	No, no, everything she touches turns to gold. No matter what. Thanks for coming.
VICTOR	We'll have to wait for your call, is that it?
BLANCHE	That's it.
VICTOR	All right. Well, we'll wait for your call.
BLANCHE	That's right, thank you.
VICTOR	Oh no, thank *you*.
	A beat.
	Nothing happens.
ETIENNE	So, let's go.
	ETIENNE moves towards the exit.
VICTOR	Ciao.
	They leave.
BLANCHE	Are you sure you don't want to use real actors?
LUCE	It's kept me up for the last two nights but now I'm sure. They're exactly what I want. They've lived through so much...they're so...alive! They'll be perfect. You're all going to be perfect, Blanche.
BLANCHE	Yeah, but I'm not sick, Luce. There's nothing wrong with me. I don't hurt anywhere.

LUCE	You've always dreamed of going back to acting.
BLANCHE	Me?
LUCE	Blanche!
BLANCHE	Come on! The last time I acted in anything, I was six months old and it was a diaper commercial.
LUCE	Blanche!
BLANCHE	And what if I'm embarrassed to appear in public?
LUCE	It's an itty bitty part.
BLANCHE	You won't come crying to me in the wings every night because you're sorry?
LUCE	I want soul, Blanche. I want it to be real.

PIPO enters wearing dark glasses.

PIPO	God Almighty, sometimes I wonder if we're actually living on the same planet!
LUCE	It's going to be a masterpiece, Pipo.
PIPO	Masterpiece or no masterpiece, have you had a good look at the part? What's the matter with you? It's not for you. There isn't an emptier, more decrepit, more sexless character in the entire repertoire. You'll look like a whipped dog. You're going to kill your image. Your public adores you, Luce. They

want to see you live, they want to see you love, hate, lie, suffer, they want you to keep them on the edge of their seats. They don't want to see you play some goddamned scraggly runt in a bloody stinking cruddy two-bit role. You're going to destroy your career, Luce!

BLANCHE   She's the talent, Pipo, she's the one who decides, not you.

PIPO   I'm the one she owes her talent to! If it hadn't been for me she wouldn't have got anywhere. If not for me she'd have ended up like all the others who waste their time wandering from place to place begging for parts only to wind up bare-assed in some porno film!

LUCE   This play is in my blood.

PIPO   Luce! For three hundred years I've fought tooth and nail for you to become somebody in this damned business! You can't throw it all away by getting on stage to do one measly speech and leaving the lead roles to two amateurs who crawled out from under a log and who don't know their asses from their elbows. What on earth is wrong with you? You need a real role, Luce!

LUCE   I'm empty, Pipo, I don't feel anything anymore, I have nothing left to give, that's the only role I can do.

PIPO   Don't you think that you'd be better off taking a little holiday instead of spending your nights turning yourself inside out and drinking yourself into oblivion? Perhaps that would screw your head on straight. Maybe then the great actress would come back to earth instead of wasting time with this preposterous escapade.

LUCE   The great actress has nothing left to give.

PIPO   We're not mounting this, Luce!

LUCE   I need to, Pipo. It'll be the role of my life, I promise you.

PIPO   Bloody hell.

LUCE   But in order for it to be what it has to be, for me to play Lucky's silence the way it must be played, for me to play the whipped dog with all my soul, I need to be on stage with the true Pozzo.

                              Pause

PIPO   You don't have the right to ask that of me, Luce.

LUCE   Yes.

PIPO   No!

LUCE   We're going to play out our lives, Pipo. We're going to show the audience the depths of our souls. We're going to make the walls speak, you in your role and me in mine! It'll be the role of your life!

PIPO	Give me a break! The day that Great Practical Joker in the sky took away my sight, it wasn't so the Oedipus he turned me into could go back and see his mother, is that clear?
BLANCHE	Well, Pozzo is blind in the second act.
LUCE	I'll guide you, as if I were your dog. All you'll have to do is hold on to the rope.
PIPO	I gave up acting. I don't act. I don't act any-more. And I will never act again.
LUCE	You won't need to act.
PIPO	I have other fish to fry besides flogging dead horses.
LUCE	You have to be there.
PIPO	No.
LUCE	If that's how you feel. Fine. Dump me. Close your eyes. Keep them closed. Blanche and I will hold up your theatre by ourselves. Until we're completely empty. No, no, never mind. Just keep letting me down!
PIPO	That's right. And when you've hit bottom, we'll talk.
LUCE	Adieu.

Piano bar.

LUCE moves over to the PIANIST.

PIPO   Balls.

BLANCHE   There are pigeons in the rafters, Pipo. What
              should we do?

PIPO   What do you *think* we should do?

              They exit, BLANCHE guiding PIPO.

LUCE   *At the piano* My soul is asleep, Nicholas, my
              soul is asleep. Somewhere deep inside of
              me. And if I want to awaken it, if I want to
              awaken my soul, I have to shatter all the
              great actress's masks. I have to plunge down
              into the bottom of the great void that's
              engulfing me. Into the heart of the
              immense silence where I struggle with
              myself like a monster to be exorcized.

              The PIANIST stops.

              Play. Keep on playing.

Scene 3

Fugue.

ETIENNE and VICTOR enter from opposite sides. They go over to the tree, stopping there while BLANCHE enters and climbs the ladder, followed by PIPO who leans on it.

Nothing happens.

ETIENNE   So, what do we do now?

VICTOR   We wait, Etienne, we wait.

ETIENNE   Meanwhile, we're bein' paid ta act, we're not bein' paid ta fuckin' wait for her!

VICTOR   Really, Etienne! Maybe we could make ourselves useful. I'm not allowed to strain—the doctor told me I could tear something—but *you* could help them to...

ETIENNE   Shit, I got enough trouble just haulin' myself around as it is. Anyways, it ain't in our contract.

VICTOR   Etienne, really.

PIPO   Some day you're going to be sorry you ever signed that contract. You'll see.

LUCE enters.

LUCE   "Have I not reason, think you, to look pale?"[1]

---

[1] William Shakespeare, *Titus Andronicus,* Act II, sc. iii.

PIPO	Great. Here we go again.
LUCE	"These two have 'ticed me hither, to this place: here never shines the sun..."
PIPO	Blanche, give her her pill.
LUCE	"Here, nothing breeds..."
PIPO	Luce, calm down.
LUCE	"And then he called me foul, adulteress, lascivious Goth, and all the bitterest terms that ever ear did hear to such effect. And had you not by wondrous fortune come, this vengeance on me had they executed."
VICTOR	Oh yes?
ETIENNE	Hnnhh.
PIPO	What's the matter with you, Luce?
LUCE	You have to do it Pipo. I'm begging you. Otherwise, I'm going to hate you forever for giving me this life.
PIPO	Now you listen to me. I don't need to exorcize my angst, do you understand? I do not *have* any angst. I am perfectly *happy*.
LUCE	*Reacting* No—not that.
PIPO	Yes, I'm happy.
LUCE	*Reacting again* Arrgh!

PIPO

And as for my soul, it's minding its own business in the wings and that's where it's going to sweat it out until I croak. And if you keep on pestering me about it I'm going to close down this barn, is that clear?

> *BLANCHE leads PIPO toward the door. He exits.*

LUCE

You wouldn't do it, I know you wouldn't do it. This place is too full of you. All those years. The walls are full of you, Pipo. You'd die. And anyway, you're aching to act. Just think...

BLANCHE

OK, that's enough.

> *BLANCHE gives LUCE her sedative. She swallows it.*

> *A beat.*

LUCE

All right. I'm sorry.

VICTOR

No no.

ETIENNE

Well...

VICTOR

Really, Etienne.

LUCE

Imagine... Imagine two men. Two old lifelong friends. Waiting. At a roadside. Beside a tree. For Godot to arrive. What do they do while they wait?

VICTOR

Well, I...

LUCE	They talk about their lives. They eat. They sleep. They fight. They make up. They talk, talk, talk. Then, at twilight, when a little boy comes to tell them that Godot isn't coming today but will surely come tomorrow—that's the role Blanche is going to play—then what do they do?
VICTOR	Well, I...
LUCE	They go off to sleep, somewhere, each one on his own. And that's the end of Act One. In Act Two, the next day, same story. The same thing happens.
ETIENNE	What happens?
LUCE	Nothing.
ETIENNE	And how long's it last?
LUCE	A whole lifetime.
BLANCHE	Two hours.
ETIENNE	Christ, that's a long time.
LUCE	That depends on you two.
VICTOR	Well, yes, really, Etienne.
LUCE	Imagine that you two are those two men. Two old lifelong friends. One lame, the other incontinent.
VICTOR	Right, I went and had the VD test this morning and it was positive.

LUCE	Good. Thank you Victor, bravo.
VICTOR	It was my pleasure.
LUCE	Where was I?
ETIENNE	It was gonna be long for nothing.
LUCE	Yes! Imagine that you had spent your whole lives waiting, that your entire lives had been lived just killing time. Do you follow me?
ETIENNE	Do I ever.
LUCE	Perfect. Now improvise it for me!

A beat.

Nothing happens.

VICTOR	You want us to improvise?
LUCE	Start whenever you're ready.
VICTOR	*Getting ready* OK.
ETIENNE	I'd rather not walk if ya don't mind.
LUCE	The important thing is that you feel the character.

ETIENNE sits down, perplexed.

A beat.

Nothing happens.

| VICTOR | They're getting bored and they've lost all hope and it's not funny but that's all there is, is that it? |
| LUCE | That's it. Just go ahead whenever you feel ready. |

A beat.

Nothing happens.

| ETIENNE | Yeah, but I don't got a clue. |
| LUCE | That's a good start. Use it and let yourself go. |

ETIENNE looks increasingly perplexed.

BLANCHE	We're waiting.
VICTOR	It's hard. He's not used to this.
LUCE	Start from who you are.

A beat.

Nothing happens.

ETIENNE	We s'posed to keep goin' like this for long?
LUCE	Just keep going. I'll tell you when to stop.
VICTOR	You'll tell us when?
BLANCHE	Yes!

A beat.

VICTOR	*Lets out a huge sigh* Ahhhhh.
LUCE	That's good Victor. That's good.
VICTOR	*Smiling, whispering* Thanks.
ETIENNE	What the hell was so good?
VICTOR	*Whispering* We're improvising now, Etienne, we're improvising.
ETIENNE	Oh.

A beat.

Nothing happens.

VICTOR *takes a deep breath.*

VICTOR	Ah oui...
ETIENNE	Hey, maybe we could put on some music.
VICTOR	Etienne, really!
ETIENNE	What?
VICTOR	I was improvising!
ETIENNE	Sorry.

A beat.

VICTOR *concentrates once again.*

VICTOR	*French accent* How are zee feet, mon ami?

ETIENNE	Don't ask. I got enough problems just tryin' ta concentrate on this acting stuff.
VICTOR	Really, Etienne.
ETIENNE	What?
VICTOR	I was improvising.
ETIENNE	Huh?
VICTOR	I was improvising!
ETIENNE	Sorry. Christ.
VICTOR	*To LUCE, calming himself* Sorry, sorry. We'll start over.

VICTOR concentrates once again.

VICTOR	*French accent* Ah yes. To kill zee time. Oui, to kill zee time. Ah, life, she is a battle.
ETIENNE	Gimme a break.
VICTOR	*Persisting* Yes! I swear to you, my good friend, mon ami, my brother, what a battle. What a confounded battle. Ah yes.
ETIENNE	Ya sound pretty weird.
VICTOR	*Yelling* Yes!
LUCE	What kind of accent is that, Victor?
VICTOR	*Meekly* Huh?

LUCE	What is that accent?
VICTOR	Oh, well... I'm sorry, it's just that when I was learning my lines I thought, seeing as the action takes place in the Macon country—I mean in France—if I want it to seem believable it's a good idea to work on the accent right away because, it's not that hard, but it still takes work. I mean the accent, right?
LUCE	The Macon country?
VICTOR	I don't know. What do you think?
LUCE	The Macon country? But the Macon country is right here.
VICTOR	Oh yes? In what sense?
LUCE	Your characters are right here, they're over there, on the corner, beside a telephone pole. Here. You're the mirror of your audience, Victor. I won't settle for an insipid little shadow of humanity to hit them between the eyes with *Godot*.
VICTOR	Ah. In that sense, well, yes, that's for sure...
LUCE	All right. We'll try something else. No talking to start off. You're waiting. And you're wondering what you're going to do. But you're running out of ideas. Your inspiration has dried up Your spirit is tired, your imagination dead.
VICTOR	Right, I like this better. I feel it more this way. Don't you, Etienne?

ETIENNE   Yeah.

LUCE   Good. Boredom overcomes you. Little by lit-
               tle. You look at each other.

                       A beat.

                       They look at each other.

               Yes, that's it. But seeing each other like that,
               abandoned to yourselves—seeing each other
               like some kind of decrepit larvae emptied of
               all their substance, is more than you can
               bear.

                       A searching look from ETIENNE.

               So, to lessen your pain, you turn away from
               each other, each in his own direction.

                       VICTOR turns. ETIENNE imitates him.

               That's right, yes. But anguish paralyses you
               completely. As if you were no longer living.

                       VICTOR freezes. ETIENNE imitates him.

               Yes! The audience should think you've gone
               blank—to the point that they wonder if the
               play has stopped. Time stands still. Everyone
               is waiting. For something to happen. For
               something to occur. For something to begin.
               You're going to tough it out until someone
               in the audience gets up.

VICTOR   Uh huh?

ETIENNE	What?!
LUCE	Yes! But at that very moment, to the surprise of the spectator who has gotten up to leave, we're going to hear them suffer.
ETIENNE	We're gonna hear them what?
VICTOR	I think she said suffer.
ETIENNE	Aww, gimme a break.
LUCE	Yes! They moan. They wail. They cry out. With all their dead voices. Go on.

VICTOR lets out a long moan.

Yes! That's it. All the pain of their existence comes out. Etienne!

VICTOR continues moaning. ETIENNE timidly joins in.

ETIENNE	Aouwe!
LUCE	Put some soul into it!

They howl louder and louder.

VICTOR	Ughhhhhhhhhh!
ETIENNE	Ahhhhhh!
LUCE	Yes! Yes! Yes! We have to feel that before any word, before any syllable, the howl is at the heart of man. Yes! Yes! Yes!

PIPO enters.

PIPO Good God! What in heaven's name is going on here?

ETIENNE Yeah—what the fuck's this all about!

PIPO Are you out of your mind?

LUCE You don't want to be here so let me do things my way.

PIPO But Luce, what you're doing is dangerous! They're going to blow their voices shrieking like that. They're not actors—they don't have trained voices, they have no technique, they have nothing.

LUCE What's the use of having a voice if you're not going to use it. I'm not interested in technique, Pipo. If you were here you'd see how much these two have lived, how they've *lived* instead of spending their lives desperately trying to be somebody else all the time. You'd see how unspoiled they are, how naive they are, how much purity there is in their slightly boyish tenderness; it would fill your soul. But no, his highness is above all that. His highness has stopped living.

PIPO Please, Luce, come on!

LUCE No no no, that's fine. I understand. There used to be a time when this theatre was full of human warmth. There used to be a time when this theatre was full of the spirit of collaboration, full of desire, solidarity...

PIPO	Luce...
LUCE	No no. That's all right. Go back to work. You have better things to do than waste your time baring your soul. We wouldn't want to let anyone see our soul, oh no! We don't want to let out all those voices gnawing away at us inside. We prefer to keep them quiet, in the wings.
PIPO	My little light.
LUCE	You have to sink pretty low to waste your time nurturing your misery for days on end just to finally put it on display. Blecch. Well that's what we're doing, Pipo. I want you to start from right where you are. It's not much, I know, but it's something. I'm not asking you to act, but to be! To be, you know what that means, don't you, to be, huh? Answer me.
VICTOR & ETIENNE	*In unison* Yes, yes. Ya ya ya.
LUCE	I want you to get as close as possible to your souls.
PIPO	Like getting close to the tree of knowledge...
LUCE	Yes. Exactly.

Piano bar.

LUCE	We have to strip everything away. Till we're completely naked. And alone. Like Adam and Eve. Naked and alone. Adieu.

LUCE goes over to the piano.

BLANCHE	Luce!
PIPO	Balls!
BLANCHE	Well!

BLANCHE goes out into the wings.

PIPO moves towards his office.

ETIENNE	What about us?
VICTOR	What *about* us?
ETIENNE	Jesus Christ! Don't tell me I came all that way this morning just for that?
VICTOR	You have to understand her—she seems so sensitive.
PIPO	If you want some advice: Leave and don't come back. There's no future for you two here.
VICTOR	But there isn't one anywhere else either.
ETIENNE	Yeah, so worry about your own problems, OK?
PIPO	I warned you.
VICTOR	Come on. We'll go think about it.
ETIENNE	About what?

VICTOR   Ah! About everything that's eating away at
                us inside. About all the human larvae that
                suck all the good out of us—about all the
                debris that buries our existence. Ah! The
                theatre! It's really something.

ETIENNE   Don't get carried away!

                        They exit.

LUCE   *At the piano* I dream of the night when my
                soul will rise up, like in the old Greek the-
                atres that open onto the sky. I dream that
                my soul starts to rise in front of the audi-
                ence, higher and higher, until it carries the
                roof away with it, rising, rising, rising...

                        The PIANIST stops.

                Play, keep on playing.

Scene 4

Fugue.

VICTOR and ETIENNE enter from opposite sides.

They move to the tree and stop there while BLANCHE enters and sits down at the sewing machine to work on the costumes. VICTOR is studying his lines in earnest. ETIENNE is fooling around, crouched over his foot.

VICTOR   Etienne!

ETIENNE   Mmmn?

VICTOR   Did you think about your soul last night while going over the day in your head?

ETIENNE   No time ta waste on that.

VICTOR   Really, Etienne, it's important to develop your imagination for the part.

ETIENNE   It'll be there just fine when it's time to get my ass on stage.

VICTOR   Anyway, I thought about mine. And if I really dig into the inner life of my character, I'd say that... It's hard to explain, but...

ETIENNE   You're such a fuckin' eager beaver, aren'tcha.

A pause.

ETIENNE	What, ya sulking?
VICTOR	Drop it.
ETIENNE	Go on, spit it out.
VICTOR	All right. Did you know that statistically speaking, guidance counsellors have proven that sixty per cent of twenty to twenty-seven-year-olds who enter college suffering from constipation or venereal disease stop laughing by the end of their first semester? Did you know that?
ETIENNE	Must make a guy feel more like one of the gang.
VICTOR	I don't know, it's like, I mean, somewhere, I mean, it's like, I don't know.
ETIENNE	You said it.
VICTOR	Jeez, it's getting scary. It's almost reached the point where *I* get lost in thought too.
ETIENNE	Meanwhile, *I'm* wasting my time here doing dick all.
BLANCHE	She's coming, she's on her way.
	Pause.
	Nothing happens.
VICTOR	All right, well, I think I'll go have a pee.
ETIENNE	You do that.

VICTOR exits and returns immediately walking backwards, face to face with LUCE.

LUCE   "You think I am weak, you think I love you, that my womb thirsted for your seed..."[1]

VICTOR   Good heavens!

LUCE   "You think I want to carry your offspring beneath my heart, nourish it with my blood...bear your child and take your name?"

VICTOR   Uh...no. No, I never said that.

LUCE   "By the way, what is your surname? I've never heard it."

VICTOR   Really.

LUCE   "Probably you haven't got one."

VICTOR   Oh, really!

ETIENNE   What's the matter? She sick?

BLANCHE   No, it's Miss Julie who's sick.

VICTOR   *Snickering* Whew. You had me scared there.

LUCE   Have you ever had the feeling, when you smile, my dear Victor, that even if your smile is stretched out to your ears for so long your facial muscles are paralyzed, people see only your soul trying to save face?

---

[1] August Strindberg, *Miss Julie,* translator's adaptation.

VICTOR	Can you repeat that? I don't think I understood.
LUCE	That's exactly what I'm looking for, Victor—for you to be able to lose face. For you to let yourself go into what you feel is the most insignificant part of yourself, and for that insignificance to become, for one evening, in front of a handful of spectators—for your insignificance as a man to become...a work of art.
VICTOR	Oh yes, I understand...
LUCE	From today on I'd like us to be totally open with each other, do you understand? Don't hold anything back.
ETIENNE	Whoa. She ain't beatin' around the bush this morning.
LUCE	Yes?
ETIENNE	Huh?
LUCE	Sorry.
ETIENNE	Oh, no problem.
LUCE	I haven't had my pill yet. Blanche.
VICTOR	Really, Etienne.
ETIENNE	I didn't say anything.

> *BLANCHE gives LUCE a sedative. LUCE swallows it.*

LUCE	All right. Let's get to work. Let's look at the beginning of the play.
VICTOR	Uh...
LUCE	Estragon is sitting centre stage and he's trying to get his boot off while Vladimir is pissing in the wings.
VICTOR	Uh, well, yes, as a matter of fact...
LUCE	Take your places and play that for me.
VICTOR	Uhhh...
BLANCHE	Something wrong, Victor?
VICTOR	No no, it's just that, it's just that, that's exactly what I was going to do, pee, I mean, and, well, I don't want to hold you up but, you'll have to excuse me, I really have to go!

A pause.

VICTOR	All right?
LUCE	We mustn't deprive ourselves of enjoying the little things in life, Victor. Go. It's lovely to watch you go.
VICTOR	Thank you so much. I'm touched you've told me that, it's encouraging. Wait for me, Luce, I'll be right back.

VICTOR exits.

LUCE	Imagine! Imagine if we could transport the audience all the way there, right into the actor's most profoundly intimate moment. Just imagine what that would be like!
ETIENNE	Where, in the can?
LUCE	Wait! Wait, Etienne, wait!
ETIENNE	Jesus, what else do you think I ever do.
LUCE	Yes, that's it! You're trying to get your boot off and you can't, all right? When he comes back, you don't answer. No matter what he says, you don't speak to him, understood?
ETIENNE	Anyways, I got nothin' to say.
LUCE	Kill the wings. Come on, follow me.
BLANCHE	What are you doing?
LUCE	Trust me.

LUCE drags BLANCHE behind the audience.

VICTOR enters.

VICTOR	Excuse me, eh, the doctor said that it's better for me to go often because... Uh...oh. What's going on here? They're gone? Etienne, really, answer me.

A beat.

All right, what's going on here?

A beat.

Ah! I get it. We're waiting for Godot, is that it?

A beat.

VICTOR's eyes seek LUCE.

Oh! She wants us to improvise? Am I ever stupid...

> *He concentrates and improvises in a falsely naturalistic tone.*

Oh! Estragon! I'm happy to see you again, I felt all alone, and being alone, I mean, all alone, is something I can't stand.

> *VICTOR stops abruptly and his eyes briefly seek LUCE.*

> *He returns to his improvisation.*

Ah, Life! Life, life... Life has no meaning when you're all alone.

> *A pause.*

Especially when there's someone else around.

> *A pause.*

Well, come on, do something, really!

> *ETIENNE is getting tired.*

	Great. That's it. It's already sneaking up on me. I'm going to have to go pee again.
LUCE	*From the audience* Piss onstage!
VICTOR	Oh! There you are! You scared me!
LUCE	Could you piss onstage, please, Victor?
VICTOR	You want me to what...?
LUCE	Let's try it.
VICTOR	Well really. Why?
LUCE	On opening night we'll have no secrets left, Victor, might as well start right now.
VICTOR	Boy, I was ready for anything except this.
LUCE	Please, do me a favour. Let yourself go.
VICTOR	Uh, okay.
	He turns his back and mimes pissing.
LUCE	No, Victor. I didn't ask you to pretend to piss, I asked you to piss. Unless you really didn't need to go that badly.
VICTOR	No, no, it's not that, but...
LUCE	Well, go on.
VICTOR	You want me to do it for real?
LUCE	That's right.

VICTOR	Well. I can't.
LUCE	You're embarrassed to show yourself.
VICTOR	It would take a lot less to embarrass me.
ETIENNE	She's not asking for your fuckin' soul. She's just asking you to take out your wad!
VICTOR	Etienne, really, please stay out of this!
LUCE	Victor!
VICTOR	But in the script, Vladimir doesn't urinate onstage. I don't see how showing myself bare-naked is going to serve the author's intention...

A beat.

I'm sorry, but I need to understand, that's how I work...

A beat.

I'd really like to, but I have a block.

LUCE	Let's get past it, Victor, all right?
VICTOR	It's not very pretty, eh. I'm warning you—it's not at all aesthetically pleasing.

A pause.

VICTOR pretends to undo his undershorts.

VICTOR	*Stopping himself* No. I'm sorry, but no.

LUCE	Fine. As you wish. Come back when you're ready. Thank you.

She exits.

VICTOR	Well really...
BLANCHE	Luce!
ETIENNE	Jesus Christ! Come on!
BLANCHE	Perhaps if we read the script, to understand the state of the characters.
ETIENNE	The state of the characters! We've been waiting for her for a fuckin' hour! We're up to our tits in the state of the characters!
VICTOR	Etienne, really. Don't listen to him, OK? He doesn't really mean that. It's my fault, I'm sorry...
ETIENNE	Don't talk if you got nothin' to say.
VICTOR	But... But...
LUCE	*Coming back onstage* The rehearsal is over, thank you.
ETIENNE	She's out of her fuckin' mind.
VICTOR	Etienne, don't say that. I'm sorry. We're sorry. Say you're sorry.
ETIENNE	Come on, wake up. She's fuckin' derailed, that's for sure.

61

ETIENNE leaves.

VICTOR   Etienne! Well, OK, see you tomorrow. OK?
Tomorrow? Ciao.

VICTOR leaves.

BLANCHE paces back and forth.

BLANCHE   What's going on, Luce? Don't you think
you're going overboard? It's great to want to
direct actors who aren't actors but maybe
you should start by knowing where you want
to lead them.

LUCE   Give me a pill.

BLANCHE   You can't rely on them—they don't know
how to do anything. You can't keep stopping
the rehearsals every time they don't give you
what you want. They don't even know what
you want. I don't either, for that matter. Do
you know what you want? Is everyone going
to be naked on stage? Hurry up and decide
because I've just started the costumes and
I'd rather not make them for nothing.

LUCE   There won't be any costumes.

BLANCHE   Piss on stage, huh? Piss on stage! Piss on
stage. Did you stop and think for one sec-
ond who would have to mop it up every
night after the show? Huh?

LUCE   I'm sorry.

A pause.

I want soul, Blanche. I want the audience to see the actors' souls. A soul, a soul, only a soul, a human soul, and what that soul expresses in all its, its... All its...

Pipo enters.

PIPO   Its what? Its what? Who do you think you are, Luce? You're not going to find the truth by rummaging through other people's garbage. Stop acting the great ethereal mad-woman!

LUCE   I'm not acting, Pipo, I'm not acting.

PIPO   For heaven's sake! We're not priests, Luce. You're going to crack up playing this game. Soul, soul! What's with you? What are you looking for? What does the soul eat in win-ter, huh Luce?

Piano bar.

LUCE goes over to the PIANIST.

BLANCHE   Luce!

PIPO   God Almighty.

BLANCHE   Come...

They exit, BLANCHE leading PIPO.

LUCE   *At the piano* It's my duty to set a goal for myself, so that I don't disappoint Blanche or Pipo or anyone, anyone on earth. And every waking hour, until opening night, I have to strive to attain that goal. It's the only way to give the word "soul" its true meaning.

The PIANIST stops.

Play. Keep on playing.

Scene 5

Fugue.

Victor and Etienne enter from opposite sides.

They go to the tree and stop there.

Victor murmurs his lines, Etienne fools around with his foot.

Nothing happens.

ETIENNE   What do we do now?

VICTOR   We wait, Etienne, we wait.

ETIENNE   Jesus Christ, she ever gonna show up?

VICTOR   I think it's a directing gimmick, to help get us on the right track.

ETIENNE   We don't have to show up here—the TV's full of goddamned preachers for that.

VICTOR   In any case, *I'm* ready. And she's not leaving here until I've shown her everything.

ETIENNE   All's I can say is if she asks for it, is she ever gonna get it.

VICTOR   Me too. I can hardly wait.

Blanche enters carrying a pair of boots for Etienne.

BLANCHE	Here, Etienne, put these on. They're Estragon's boots.
ETIENNE	I don't want to upset you, but they're too small.
BLANCHE	You'll have to make do. Luce wanted them to be too small.
ETIENNE	Mine are bigger and they already hurt.
BLANCHE	*Sitting at the table* Just scrunch up your toes.
ETIENNE	Just suck me off.

ETIENNE puts the boots on.

BLANCHE busies herself at the table.

VICTOR	Ah! What we wouldn't do for the theatre, Etienne, huh? Ah! The theatre! The theatre! It's a whole other world, the theatre. The admiring audience, the flowers, the make-up, the costumes, the sets, the rounds of applause, the curtain coming down on laughter and tears, the frenzy in the wings, and the long nights after the show drinking and carousing with fellow actors. Ah, the theatre! The theatre! Ah! I feel alive, I feel truly alive. I'm ecstatic, Etienne, I'm truly in heaven!
ETIENNE	They don't fit.
VICTOR	Really, Etienne! What I was just saying was poetic, wasn't it?

ETIENNE	They don't fit. They don't fit, fuckin' shit!
VICTOR	You have to suffer to be somebody, and life isn't always a bed of roses, Etienne.
ETIENNE	*Sitting back down* What's up your ass this morning?
VICTOR	I don't know, I get lyrical when I think about the new life opening up in front of me now that I've broken through my inner blocks. Just think of all the parts—all the lives—I'm going to be given!
ETIENNE	Go to hell!
VICTOR	Really.

A beat.

Nothing happens.

LUCE enters, drunk.

ETIENNE	Oh oh. Looks like someone got shitfaced last night.
LUCE	*To ETIENNE* Gimme 20 bucks. The taxi's waiting at the door.
ETIENNE	What play did she walk outta this time?
LUCE	Come on, gimme me 20 bucks!

BLANCHE goes off to PIPO's office.

ETIENNE	Ain't got a red cent ta my name.

LUCE	I'll remember that!

BLANCHE exits to PIPO's office.

VICTOR	Maybe we could all chip in.

LUCE	Pipo! Gimme 20 bucks!

BLANCHE returns.

BLANCHE	Oh Lord.

LUCE	Gimme my pill, Blanche.

BLANCHE	Just hold your horses.

BLANCHE exits hurriedly.

LUCE	That's it! Wait! Just you wait, all of you. When I die, I won't forget you. In my will I'm gonna give you a pile of things I don't have, just to show you how you gave me nothing—when I spent my life sacrificing body and soul and milking myself dry to give you every last drop of me like the lowest of the low. Just you wait!

BLANCHE returns.

BLANCHE	I hope you're proud of yourself.

LUCE	Don't yell at me—the taxi went to the wrong theatre three times.

BLANCHE	You have a show to get up, Luce! We've been waiting for you for four hours!

LUCE	I'm sorry! I'm sorry! I'm sorry! I'm sorry!

BLANCHE exits.

ETIENNE	Fuck being sorry. You just don't do stuff like that!
VICTOR	Etienne, really!
ETIENNE	I got no more time to waste here than any-where else.
VICTOR	Really, Etienne!
LUCE	Hmm! Etienne! My handsome Etienne! Don't despair, you won't have waited for nothing, trust me. You don't know what I've got in store for you this morning, Etienne. And I'm not just anybody either. I may be starting to sink pretty low, but I'm still not dirt and don't you forget it! Did I take my pill? Yes. OK.
BLANCHE	OK. Take your places.
VICTOR	Uh... I have something important to share with you this morning.
LUCE	This morning, I think the important thing is going to be Etienne, this morning.
VICTOR	Yes, yes, but...
LUCE	No no... Our poor Etienne hasn't waited all this time for nothing.
VICTOR	Yes, but—

LUCE	No!
VICTOR	I'm sorry.
LUCE	Let's get started. Etienne, you're all alone on stage.
ETIENNE	And my feet hurt like hell.
LUCE	That's it. Then you sit down, then you take off your boots. Go on, play it out for me.
ETIENNE	I can see you comin' a mile away. Check this out!

> *He struggles and struggles with his boot, in vain.*

Oh Christ!

LUCE	That's it, yes. Harder.
ETIENNE	Jesus Christ!
LUCE	Harder!
ETIENNE	No point, goddammit, it's jammed in there.
LUCE	How does it feel?
ETIENNE	Whaddya mean, how does it feel?
VICTOR	She's asking if it hurts, I think.
ETIENNE	Does the Pope shit in the woods?
LUCE	All right. Let's start from there. Let's continue. Try to take off your boot.

ETIENNE	*Trying again* Fuckin' Jesus!
LUCE	Go on. Give it everything you've got.
ETIENNE	*Trying with all his might* You satisfied? Huh?
LUCE	It's your whole life, Etienne. Imagine—
ETIENNE	I don't have to imagine anything, it's all there already.
LUCE	Imagine that your whole life you've had your feet crammed into boots that were too small.
ETIENNE	*Out of strength* Fuck!
LUCE	And you've never managed to get them off.
ETIENNE	Hey...
LUCE	Do you feel the character?
ETIENNE	Up to my ass.
LUCE	What can save him?
ETIENNE	Save him from what?
LUCE	From his pain!
ETIENNE	Getting his boot off, goddammit!
LUCE	But if he can't!
ETIENNE	Then there's nothing he can do. He lives with it and toughs it out.

71

LUCE	But Etienne, what can save you?
ETIENNE	Nothin', I said.
LUCE	No, there must be something that will save you or else you'll be stuck in those boots until you're sixty-five.
ETIENNE	Go to hell, bitch!

ETIENNE pushes LUCE.

VICTOR	Etienne!
ETIENNE	At sixty-five I won't have any fuckin' feet left! I'll be dragging myself around like the leg-less gimp in front of the Salvation Army.
LUCE	The legless gimp?
ETIENNE	In front of the Sally Ann, yeah. He's slumped on the sidewalk, filthy as all hell, and he sucks his fingers like a two-month-old baby. Is that deep enough in the shit for ya?
VICTOR	Really, Etienne!
ETIENNE	What! That's where I come from and that's where I'll fuckin' end up!
LUCE	But why does he suck his fingers?
ETIENNE	He looks after them so that they'll keep cartin' him around. He does it like this.

ETIENNE sucks his thumb.

LUCE	Yes! That's it! Do it for me! Go on!

Bass piano notes.

ETIENNE	*Acting* "Ya see that there, I just finished suckin' my left thumb. Now, I make a mark on it so's I remember that's the one I've just done. Like that. And I move on to another finger. You see, that one there, he's up to six marks. That means I move to the other one who doesn't have so many marks. Watch real good. Him there, he's up to six. Him too. That one too. Himtoo himtoo himtoo himtoo. That means the hand goes in my pocket. Now, I can move on to the other hand. Yes ma'am! I gotta suck 'em equal, ya understand? I spend all day long takin' care o' them fingers of mine. Hey! It ain't easy ta get around in life when you got nothin' but two flabby and flaccid stumps a leg that ain't worth shit, 'cause they done nothing for years! I need my fingers ta get around, d'ya understand?"

ETIENNE leaps up, enraged.

The day my fingers give out on me, all I want is to fall flat on my face once and for all and spread out in a heap. Ta be nothin' but a heap and not even be able to crawl. And for all I care the pile can get covered with dust and flies waitin' for the winter and the snow blower ta send it flyin' to the four corners of the earth. Now get off my case.

Long silence.

LUCE	Yes. That's it, Etienne, that's it. Yes. That's it, Estragon.
VICTOR	Oh yes! That's good Etienne. It's very very good. Very good. It's touching. Hmm. Uh... And me too, actually, I feel ready to reveal myself too.

He climbs on a chair.

Low music.

And shows them his member.

Does that have enough soul for you?

LUCE	My poor Victor...
BLANCHE	But it's black!
VICTOR	What's left of it.
BLANCHE	But it's dreadful!
VICTOR	It really makes a statement, huh?
BLANCHE	But it looks like it's dead!
VICTOR	Oh no, don't worry, it's very much alive, I still have a lot of feeling. No, but it's really something, isn't it?
BLANCHE	But we can't let the audience see that!
VICTOR	Me, uff, it doesn't bother me anymore. If it makes you happy—I mean, if it'll do the trick.

LUCE	I'm sorry, I'm afraid you're killing what little remains of my zest for life.
	Silence.
	Aren't you two afraid that playing this little game will kill your zest for life?
ETIENNE	Huh?
VICTOR	Oh no. That's not my style. Now I'm more the type who comes to terms with himself.
LUCE	Perhaps it's not very humane of me to ask you to reveal your little disasters to the world. I know it's difficult for you to be what you are. But do I have the right to present you to the world as though you were the dregs of humanity?
VICTOR	It's not insignificant enough, is that it? Maybe we can find something else.
LUCE	No, thank you, it's too much. I'm sorry but I wasn't expecting this. I think the time has come to thank you for having been here. Yes, thank you. You've been generous. I would have liked us to become friends. But you can't command friendship. It has to answer something one has inside. And it turns out I have nothing. Thank you very much.
BLANCHE	Oh shit! Luce, please!
VICTOR	Uh, but... but it's not over for good, not forever?

ETIENNE	What the fuck's the matter with her? Ya put your cock on the table, I mean, you put your ass on the line and it ends there. Come on now! What's the problem? What's goin' on in that head o' yours? Do you think I'm a hunk of meat that you can shove around all over the place like I was your performing dog? I got a contract right here, OK? That means you're gonna get your act together and tell me what to do so that Mr. Shades coughs up the dough, and as for your fancy-schmantzy psychology and this pulling the plug business, you can roll them up tight and shove them up you know where, that's what I think, OK? It ain't me who's the disaster here!
VICTOR	That's enough, Etienne, really! She had a moment of real emotion there, didn't she?
ETIENNE	Who does she think she is?
VICTOR	Well... She's a great actress.
ETIENNE	She might be a great actress, but she doesn't cut it as a human being, if you want my opinion!
VICTOR	Etienne, really, am I going to have to start swearing to get you to stop humiliating me like this left and right!
ETIENNE	Go ahead!
VICTOR	Darn it!
BLANCHE	OK, OK, that's enough. Thank you for coming, go home now.

76

VICTOR	But—but it wasn't me!
BLANCHE	I'll call you if we need you.
VICTOR	But he was the one...!
ETIENNE	Come on, let's get out of here, otherwise I'm fuckin' gonna end up biting her!

ETIENNE leaves.

VICTOR	But—what about me!
ETIENNE	*In the wings* Will you haul your fuckin' ass!

A pause.

VICTOR	Well uh... See you tomorrow? We'll see each other tomorrow. Don't you worry. We'll get through this together. You can count on Etienne and I. We'll all end up trusting each other. You'll see. I like you very much. Ciao!

He exits.

BLANCHE	All right, listen to me now. We're going to roll up our sleeves, we're going to get our act together like we're supposed to and we're going to take the bull by the horns, OK?
LUCE	I don't know what I'm doing any more, Blanche.
BLANCHE	Well, so, let's start from there—let's try to see things a little more clearly, OK? OK. We have a script. Tomorrow, we're going to start

by reading it. We are not going to wonder exactly where it hurts and whether it hurts a lot or if it hurts too much. It's pointless, that's where you get lost, Luce. We're going to read the play, *that's it, that's all.* Of course, that's if Etienne knows how to read. Well, let's say he knows how to read. Let's not. Let's imagine the worst, let's say he doesn't know how to read. So then, I'll teach him his lines. But that means we can't do a readthrough tomorrow. All right. You see, things are already a bit clearer. If you decided to block the scenes, that would be a start, wouldn't it?

LUCE   I don't know I don't know, I don't know anymore. I'm tired.

BLANCHE   We'll find a solution.

                PIPO enters.

PIPO   I know what we're going to do. We're going to cancel. At least that way you'll save face!

LUCE   If you acted with me, Pipo, like before... We'll play just one night if you want. If you do it with me, I promise you, I'll give it my all and I'll blow the roof off this goddamned place.

PIPO   I'm giving you until tomorrow to find your actor, otherwise I'm cancelling.

LUCE   But how do you want me to feel what I'm playing? How do you want me to give them as much as they give me, if you aren't there

	to live it with me? I'm empty, Pipo. If you're not there I can't give them anything.
PIPO	No, Luce.
LUCE	The day you had to face the fact that your career was over, the day the great actor needed someone to help him fill his huge void, who was there to raise you up?
PIPO	I'm sorry. I don't know what I'm saying anymore.
BLANCHE	Hey, whoa there, OK, whoa! That's enough. It's not the first time we've been in deep shit!
PIPO	No, but this is the deepest it's ever been.
BLANCHE	She doesn't know what she's doing anymore. She needs help.
LUCE	*Whispering* I don't know what I'm saying, I don't even know what I'm saying anymore...

She heads towards the PIANIST.

BLANCHE	Don't go. Luce! We'll find something! Oh Lord!
PIPO	For Christ's sake! Did she take her sedative?
BLANCHE	No.
PIPO	Get her back here!
BLANCHE	No, leave her, let her go. Let her get a bit of air.

Piano bar.

They exit, BLANCHE guiding PIPO.

LUCE   *At the piano* Maybe Pipo is right. Maybe the soul, the soul, doesn't exist. The soul doesn't exist! The soul doesn't exist! The soul doesn't exist!

Silence.

The PIANIST continues with Gershwin's "Summertime."

Cynical "Oh your daddy's rich And your ma is good lookin'."

The PIANIST stops.

Play. Keep on playing.

Scene 6

Fugue.

ETIENNE and VICTOR enter from opposite sides.

They go to the tree and stop there.

Nothing happens.

ETIENNE   So, what do we do now?

VICTOR   We wait, Etienne, we simply wait. Nicely and quietly.

ETIENNE   *Sitting down* Christ, there's some people who need a good kick in the ass to get them moving.

VICTOR   Don't say that, you're getting all worked up for nothing.

BLANCHE enters holding three bowler hats.

BLANCHE   All right. While we're waiting you're going to rehearse the scene where they try on the hats, that way we won't waste any time.

VICTOR   Wow! All right!

ETIENNE   I ain't budgin' from this spot till she gets here.

BLANCHE   Hey! You've still got a long way to go, so move your butt.

ETIENNE	Fuck you.
VICTOR	Come on, it'll help pass the time. You'll see, it's really easy. I'll show you, I've learned it by heart. OK. You're wearing yours and I'm wearing mine. Is that right? Yes, that's it. OK.

VICTOR puts a hat on ETIENNE's head and one on his own.

Now that one, that's Lucky's. It's on the ground. Let's say it's there. Now I pick it up, now I ask you to hold mine. You'll see, it's easy. Every time I give you one of the hats, you take yours off and you give it to me and you put the other one on your head instead of the other one, OK?

ETIENNE	Christ, this is a waste of time.
VICTOR	Watch. You take my hat and I put Lucky's on instead. Now, *you* put *my* hat on instead of yours while I see if Lucky's fits me better. Is that right? Yes, that's it. Now you put my hat on instead of yours and give me yours. Now I take yours while you see if mine fits you better. Now I exchange yours and Lucky's and give you his. You take it. Don't get discouraged. Now I see whether yours would fit me better while you put Lucky's on and give mine back. Now I take my hat back. You see if Lucky's fits you better than mine. Is that it? Yes, that's right. Now I put mine back on and give you back yours. You take yours back while I see if mine fits me better than the other two. You do the same. Now you put yours back on instead of Lucky's and you

give Lucky's to me. I take it while you check to see if yours fits you better than the other two, and I put Lucky's hat back on. Now, the hats have all gone around once. We start over again. We do it three times and at the end—tada—we freeze. Since we've been so brilliant the audience starts to clap with all their might. You'll see, it brings the house down every time. And it's easy, just like a wheel turning. Isn't it fun? So let's rehearse it to see how it goes.

ETIENNE   Do you realize we're scrapin' the bottom of the barrel? Jesus fuckin' Christ!

           PIPO enters.

PIPO   We've been waiting for nothing. She just called and said she's not coming till tomorrow.

BLANCHE   What happened?

PIPO   She's fallen in love.

BLANCHE   Shit!

ETIENNE   Fuck!

VICTOR   Oh! She must be so passionate!

BLANCHE   She'll come back, don't worry.

ETIENNE   I don't care but I'm telling you, tomorrow I'm not coming because I'm gonna fall in love with my pillow, OK?

VICTOR	Really, Etienne.
ETIENNE	What! Hell, if I'm gonna waste my time, might as well be jerking off all alone in my bed.
VICTOR	Etienne, really.
ETIENNE	Come on, let's go. Nothin' left for us to do here.
VICTOR	Wait! We'll do it one last time.
ETIENNE	I'm gettin' out of here.
VICTOR	It'll seem less like we came for nothing. And it's warm here, that's already something. Anyway, where else would you go?
ETIENNE	Shit.

ETIENNE collapses on the chair.

BLANCHE	Tell her you'll be in it, Pipo. You just have to tell her: one night. She'll act with you once and for all and we'll be done with it.
PIPO	What did she look like yesterday? She hadn't slept, eh? What was she wearing? How did she look, Blanche?
BLANCHE	When she got to rehearsal she was more of a wreck than I'd ever seen her, but when you talked about cancelling, that finished her off. You should have seen her eyes, Pipo. Tell her you're going to do it.

PIPO	It's the sedatives, Blanche. If you'd given her a pill when you saw what she looked like, we wouldn't be in this situation.
BLANCHE	It's obvious your fake sedatives aren't working.
PIPO	It keeps her morale up! We're losing her!
BLANCHE	Promise me that when she comes back tomorrow you'll tell her you're going to do it.
PIPO	I can't. I can't do it.
	Silence.
	There's no future for anybody here.
VICTOR	Why are you saying that? You shouldn't say that. It doesn't do anyone any good to hear things like that. It never has. Never.
	Several beats.
	Nothing happens.
	So, uh, what do we do now?
BLANCHE	For now, the important thing is to keep busy. I'm going to get the pigeons out.
VICTOR	Hey, great! Etienne and I will help you. Right, Etienne?
	BLANCHE climbs the ladder.

VICTOR goes over to support it.

Come on, Etienne, it'll help pass the time.
Etienne... *To* BLANCHE So?

BLANCHE   It's full of snow but I don't see any pigeons.

VICTOR   *With exaggerated delight* Wow!

PIPO   It's full of what?

VICTOR   She said it's full of snow.

BLANCHE   No, there aren't any pigeons up here. They
            must have drowned—it's full of water.

VICTOR   Ooh!

PIPO   It's full of what?

VICTOR   She said it's full of water.

ETIENNE   What, is he deaf too?

BLANCHE   No. Not a pigeon in sight.

VICTOR   *With exaggerated disappointment* Aww.

            BLANCHE descends, weary.

            A beat. Nothing happens.

            VICTOR coos like a pigeon.

VICTOR   Ooh! There is *so* one.

BLANCHE   No there isn't.

86

VICTOR	There is so! It's over there. Look—it's coming out!
BLANCHE	Well, what do you know.
VICTOR	Ooh! The nice pigeon! Ooh! Look at the nice pigeon! Catch it!
	Chase music.
BLANCHE	Catch it!
	VICTOR and BLANCHE start chasing an imaginary pigeon.
PIPO	Blanche, what's going on? What is this bullshit?
VICTOR	Catch it! Catch it!
ETIENNE	Oh come on, where?
PIPO	Blanche!
VICTOR	Come on Etienne, it'll help pass the time!
BLANCHE	*Insistent* Catch it!
PIPO	What the hell is going on here?
ETIENNE	Where do you guys see a pigeon?
VICTOR	There it is, it's over there now!
BLANCHE	Catch it!
ETIENNE	Oh get out, where?

PIPO	Blanche! Are you pulling my leg?
VICTOR	Ooh! How time flies when you're having fun!
BLANCHE	Catch it!
ETIENNE	Oh come on, Jeezus!
PIPO	Hey!

Silence

	Do you take me for a moron? If there was a pigeon in here apart from the four of us, I'd hear it.
ETIENNE	Yeah, what the fuck's this all about?
VICTOR	Well, it helped pass the time, didn't it?
ETIENNE	The goddamn time would've passed anyway.
PIPO	It's no use, Blanche.

PIPO exits.

BLANCHE	Pipo... Pipo...

BLANCHE exits.

VICTOR	All right. Let's start over. Here. This is yours and this is mine. And this is Lucky's. It's on the ground, let's say there. OK. I pick it up and ask you to hold mine.
ETIENNE	Come on. We're getting out of here. I'm not waitin' any more.

88

He exits.

VICTOR   Etienne. We could do it one last time couldn't we? OK. Well, ciao.

He puts the hats down on the table.

Ah, the theatre.

He exits.

Scene 7

Funeral march.

Luce is drunk. She saunters from the piano to the centre of the stage.

LUCE
Come on, we're going to play at Pozzo and Lucky. Tell me to dance, Pipo. Say: Dance, my little one, dance! Sing! Act! Act for me! Act in my place! Act! Act! Act!

She collapses on the ground.

Silence.

Pipo enters.

PIPO
My sweet little light...

LUCE
Your little light is being snuffed out.

PIPO
Luce...

LUCE
All living things, so many lives are being snuffed out.

PIPO
No, Luce...

LUCE
So many lives, Pipo. So many lives that give you the impression of being someone, of being alive, making up stories, thinking you're somebody... Even if in the end this is as far as you get.

PIPO
You're an actress, Luce! Your life is acting. Your life is filling yourself with other people's lives! No one gives a damn about the

rest! No one is interested in your emptiness! Not yours, or mine or anybody else's!

LUCE   But that's all I have left! Of everything you gave me, that's all I have left.

PIPO   That's not true! We always start from nothing when we act, Luce. What's difficult is getting somewhere from there. The difficult thing is making everything live, Luce. Not letting it all die. The hardest thing is not losing sight of your dreams. Not becoming cynical and pulling everything into little pieces. Of course we act, Luce, all we do is act! We tell each other stories, we scare each other, we make things up, we wring our hearts for months. We turn ourselves inside out to feel everything, grasp everything, take everything and then give it all back. And so one night you're a king, the next you're a passionate lover, and the next night you're someone else, then someone else, anyone at all! And when the story's over, you wonder what truth there was in it, your cardboard crown on your head, perfume on your cheek from the woman you've kissed a hundred times whom you absolutely loathe. Don't you see! Of course we're never as large as the destinies we play, Luce! We're nothing more than beggars of roles! But we sure as hell have to find some way of giving ourselves the impression we exist. I gave you my theatre, Luce! I gave you my whole life, grinding away like a mole in my hole, having play after play read to me to find parts worthy of your talent, busting my ass so you'd have something better than rags to wear when you played the great roles, worrying myself sick when the seats were empty and there was no money coming in because we had risked mounting what you wanted without any concessions to the culture-mongers we rub shoulders with. Is that what you're blaming me for, Luce? Would you rather I had just given it all up when my own life made me want to bury myself in my hole? Would you rather I had sold my theatre and spent the rest of my life quietly licking my wounds and listening to the time pass?

A pause.

PIPO All happiness, Luce...

LUCE moans.

Yes, all happiness comes from the game we play to give ourselves the impression we exist.

LUCE Then play with me, Pipo. Act with me.

PIPO All right. But we're going to act, Luce. All we're going to do is act. The play, nothing but the play. The role, nothing but the role, one scene after the other until the end. As you've done your whole life. And when its over, it'll be over. We'll move on to something else without asking ourselves if what we do is useful or not. Luce, we can't live in a world where people think the beauty of what we do is useless.

Funeral march. PIPO exits.

92

ETIENNE and VICTOR meet downstage centre.

ETIENNE   That morning, faithful to habit, Etienne asked Victor to come and meet him beside the tree in the little Jewish cemetery across from the theatre.

VICTOR   So, at exactly five minutes to nine, along came Victor. But when he arrived, Etienne wasn't there.

ETIENNE   In fact, Etienne had arrived ten minutes before they were supposed to meet. He had waited five minutes and since Victor was nowhere in sight, he left to take a walk on the other side of the cemetery.

VICTOR   Thinking he was the first one there and that Etienne hadn't arrived yet, Victor left after five minutes to go to the corner for a take-out coffee. When he returned, fifteen minutes later, Etienne still wasn't there.

ETIENNE   Meanwhile, Etienne had already been back. But he left again five minutes later when he realized that he had forgotten the milk and sugar that he always puts in his take-out coffee.

VICTOR   So Victor, who had been waiting for five minutes, left once again, thinking that Etienne surely hadn't gone to the theatre all alone but probably decided to get a coffee on the other side of the cemetery and he went off to catch him on the way back.

93

ETIENNE	But they didn't meet up.
VICTOR	Actually, what you have to realize is that on the other side of the little Jewish cemetery there are two places to get take-out coffee.
ETIENNE	One on the east side.
VICTOR	The other on the west.
ETIENNE	Which means that when they ended up meeting...
VICTOR	It was ten to one.

They go over to the tree.

PIPO and BLANCHE enter.

A beat.

LUCE   Let's get to work.

The actors all run around the stage, in a whirlwind of rehearsal activity.

Rehearse. Rehearse. Rehearse. Rehearse, rehearse, rehearse. A hundred times the same gestures, a hundred times the same words, a hundred times the same bits, repeated over and over and over for days and days and days on end. Everyone searching for their character. Time goes by and people work. Ecstatic, they thrive on it from morning till night. And they get high on the beauty of the characters who come to life. And they get drunk with the desire to perform.

She becomes delirious.

Rehearse. Rehearse. Rehearse. A hundred times the same gestures, a hundred times the same words, a hundred times the same bits, repeated over and over and over for days and days and days on end. Everyone searching for their character. Time goes by and people work. Ecstatic, they thrive on it from morning till night. And they get high on the beauty of the characters who come to life. And they get drunk with the desire to perform.

> *The rehearsals push on, frenetic, until all halt in silence.*

Why do we spend all our lives chasing ghosts?

> *She exits.*

Scene 8

*The wings, legs and rear curtain are in
place. The characters move to the wings.*

BLANCHE Standby, three minutes. We're starting in
three.

She exits.

VICTOR Ah! The theatre! Huh, Etienne, the theatre!

ETIENNE I don't want to upset you, but there isn't
gonna be a show, Victor!

*BLANCHE enters holding a bunch of
carnations.*

BLANCHE Standby, three minutes.

ETIENNE Three minutes my ass. You'll see. There isn't
gonna be a fuckin' show.

BLANCHE Hey. No nonsense from you.

ETIENNE I'm not settin' foot on that stage till I have
her in front of me, ya got that?

BLANCHE Hey! She goes on at 8:15 and you open the
show at 8:00 so don't ask for trouble 'cause
you're going to get it, understood!

ETIENNE Calm the fuck down.

VICTOR You know very well she's making us wait just
to create the right atmosphere.

BLANCHE	Here. These are from your mother.
VICTOR	Oh no! Don't tell me my mother's here!
BLANCHE	Now you've seen them so I can throw them out.
VICTOR	But, really, why?
BLANCHE	They're carnations!
VICTOR	So they're carnations, what's the problem?
BLANCHE	The problem is the minute there's a carnation inside a theatre something terrible happens. And if you don't get those out of here this second I don't know what I'll do to you.

She leaves.

VICTOR	All right, all right!!
ETIENNE	Really, Victor.
VICTOR	I didn't know. How was I supposed to know?

VICTOR exits with the flowers.

BLANCHE enters and starts to do PIPO's make-up.

PIPO	Well?
BLANCHE	Nothing. I called every bar in town. No one's seen her.
PIPO	Damn.

BLANCHE	Don't worry, she'll show up.

ETIENNE enters.

ETIENNE	We're being screwed around here, we've been made asses of from day one.
BLANCHE	She'll be here, she always shows up in the end.
ETIENNE	Ya, but by the time she gets here the show'll be over, just wait and see!
BLANCHE	It's not the first time she's been late.
ETIENNE	We're stuck here for eternity. Fuck.
PIPO	She gets her kicks by making me worry, is that it?
BLANCHE	That's right. Hold still.
PIPO	She'll be the death of me.
BLANCHE	Hold still.
PIPO	She has no right to do this to me.
BLANCHE	Come on, she wouldn't do that to you, you know very well she wouldn't.
PIPO	Balls!

VICTOR enters.

VICTOR	It's full! It's packed! It's jam-packed with people!

ETIENNE	At least we won't be the only suckers who came for nothin'.
VICTOR	I think I'm going to be sick.
BLANCHE	Well hurry up, we're starting in two minutes.
ETIENNE	Take your time. Ya got the whole night ahead a ya.
VICTOR	Etienne, really, stop fooling around, that's enough.
ETIENNE	We came for nothing, Victor, don't you realize?
VICTOR	Stop it, don't say that, all right, don't say that. Come on, let's find a quiet place to get centred.
ETIENNE	We got the rest of our lives ta do that.
VICTOR	Don't say that! My whole future's at stake tonight—this isn't the time to destroy all my hopes.
ETIENNE	It's gonna happen sooner or later.
VICTOR	I'm begging you!
BLANCHE	Hey! Listen, you two. If you don't want this to be the last time you ever act in front of an audience, you know what you have to do, huh?

A pause.

PIPO   Do you know what you have to do?

VICTOR   Yeah yeah.

ETIENNE   Do I ever.

VICTOR   Etienne, pleeease.

PIPO   Breathe, huh, remember to breathe!

ETIENNE   We know, will ya fuckin' relax!

                        A pause.

BLANCHE   So, well, break a leg.

VICTOR   Break a leg.

PIPO   Break a leg.

VICTOR   Break a leg.

PIPO   Break a leg.

BLANCHE   Break a leg, Etienne.

ETIENNE   Yeah, right, great! We're all gonna fuckin'
              end up with broken legs.

VICTOR   Come on, come.

                  VICTOR and ETIENNE exit.

BLANCHE   Hold still so I can finish you up.

                  ETIENNE and VICTOR enter.

VICTOR	You're ready, right?
ETIENNE	I don't want to upset you, but I don't remember a thing.
VICTOR	Oh really, Etienne!
ETIENNE	I don't know when I come on, I don't know when I go off, I don't know when I get up, or when I sit down, I don't fuckin' remember anything at all!
VICTOR	Etienne, I really don't need this right now.
ETIENNE	Get this: if we go on, get this: The pigeons are gonna shit on our heads.
VICTOR	Really, Etienne.
ETIENNE	Anyways, if we look like jerks, it's not so bad. Our names aren't even in the program.
VICTOR	Speak for yourself. My mother is out there.
ETIENNE	Anyways, I'm telling ya now, if she doesn't get onstage in time, I'm dumpin' everything and tellin' everyone ta fuckin' shove it!
VICTOR	Etienne, really. You can't do that!
ETIENNE	I'm gonna tell them that we've all been made fuckin' asses of!
VICTOR	Etienne, you don't have the right!
ETIENNE	You'll see.

VICTOR	Etienne, I'm begging you!
ETIENNE	You'll see, goddammit!
VICTOR	Etienne!

VICTOR stomps on ETIENNE's foot.

ETIENNE	Ayaaayyy!
VICTOR	You made me panic!
ETIENNE	You asked for it. I won't be able to act anymore.
VICTOR	You happy now, huh?
ETIENNE	Ya, I'm happy!
VICTOR	Oh, you're happy?
ETIENNE	Ya, I'm happy!
VICTOR	This isn't the time!
ETIENNE	Bet you're proud of yourself for having dragged me into this mess, huh? You must feel great!
VICTOR	I'm sorry, OK, I'm sorry.
ETIENNE	Goddamn motherfuckin' cocksuckin' life.
VICTOR	I apologize, Etienne, forgive me!
ETIENNE	I knew I should've gotten fuckin' smashed, dammit. I should've pickled my brain to

forget that it's me here out there makin' an ass of myself!

VICTOR   This is hardly the time, Etienne!

> *A beat.*

> *VICTOR opens his arms to embrace ETIENNE.*

Break a leg, Etienne, break a leg, OK?

> *They hug.*

> *A pause.*

Go on, dammit!

ETIENNE   Jesus fuckin' Christ!

> *He exits.*

VICTOR   Oh maaaaaa.

> *He crosses himself.*

PIPO   I feel as though I'm about to die.

BLANCHE   Don't worry, it'll go well. They'll pull it off like real pros. You have the pipe?

PIPO   Yes.

BLANCHE   Tobacco?

PIPO   Yes.

BLANCHE	Matches?
PIPO	Yes.
BLANCHE	When you light up, you'll be careful not to burn yourself, OK?
PIPO	Yes yes.
BLANCHE	The watch?
PIPO	Yes.
BLANCHE	Handkerchief?
PIPO	Yes.
BLANCHE	Whip?
PIPO	Thank you.

She gets the whip for him.

BLANCHE	Here. You always whip downstage so you don't hit anyone, OK?
PIPO	Yeah yeah.
BLANCHE	When you want to sit down, walk straight ahead. The chair will be there.
PIPO	Yeah yeah, I know, Blanche, I know!

BLANCHE holds out the rope.

BLANCHE	Here.

PIPO hesitates a moment, then takes it.

A beat.

PIPO   Do you remember when there was so much to be done in this theatre, Blanche? When everything was possible, nothing could stop us.

BLANCHE   Pipo, please.

PIPO   We're calling it off, Blanche, she's not coming.

A beat.

I'm going to speak to the audience.

BLANCHE   You're afraid to go on, is that it?

PIPO   We're stopping it right now.

BLANCHE   No!

A pause.

It's time to act, Pipo. It's time to jump in with both feet and go all the way. Without looking back. OK, maybe she's half drunk, maybe she's wandering around lost in some back alley or God knows where, wondering if the show is tonight or if it was last night or... I don't know. But what I do know is she'll show up in the end like she always does, 'cause she knows we're both here, and she knows we're waiting for her. And when she gets here I don't want to tell her we've called it off 'cause we were afraid she wouldn't come. I'm not going to let her down. Not me. I've never let her down and I'm not going to start tonight.

PIPO Tonight it's all over, Blanche.

BLANCHE Break a leg, Pipo. Go on.

She exits.

Off OK, places.

PIPO It's all over.

He sits down.

It's all over now.

Fugue, muffled and heavy.

VICTOR and ETIENNE enter upstage from either side. They make their way centre stage.

VICTOR *Lyrical* So Etienne and Victor made their entrance. And started to act.

ETIENNE *Disgusted* Etienne put his whole soul into trying to get his boot off.

VICTOR And Victor abandoned his life to become his character.

ETIENNE And when Pipo was supposed to enter with Luce.

VICTOR	When Pozzo was supposed to let out a cry to announce his entrance with Lucky.
ETIENNE	They were...

Silence

VICTOR	They were...waiting for Godot.
ETIENNE	They were waiting.
VICTOR	For something to happen.
ETIENNE	For something to begin.
VICTOR	Imagine.
ETIENNE	Imagine two men.
VICTOR	Two old lifelong friends.
ETIENNE	Waiting.
VICTOR	Beside a tree.
ETIENNE	For Godot to arrive.
VICTOR	Imagine two old friends...
ETIENNE	Their spirits tired.
VICTOR	Their imaginations dead.
ETIENNE	Imagine...

They turn their backs to each other.

ETIENNE sits. VICTOR remains standing, frozen.

A long beat.

VICTOR starts to moan softly. He moans louder and louder.

VICTOR	Ahhhh!
ETIENNE	What do we do now, eh?
VICTOR	Huh?
ETIENNE	I'm asking ya, whadda we do now?
VICTOR	Well... We wait, Estragon, we wait.
ETIENNE	Ya, well I got the feeling we're waitin' for nothin'.
VICTOR	We're not, Estragon, we're not! Go on, act, keep on acting.
ETIENNE	Wake up, Victor, she's not comin'! She isn't comin'!
VICTOR	*Panicking* Ah life! Life is a battle, Estragon. Life is an infinite battle... Ah!
ETIENNE	Come on, let's get outta here, nothin' for us ta do here.
VICTOR	Etienne!
ETIENNE	It's over, Victor.

VICTOR	No.
ETIENNE	It's over, it's all over.
VICTOR	Etienne, stop it.
ETIENNE	Whaddya want us ta do? Keep on waitin'?
VICTOR	Etienne, please.
ETIENNE	Ya want us ta stay stuck here for all eternity?
VICTOR	Etienne, I'm begging you.
ETIENNE	Waitin' for a goddamn nutcase...
VICTOR	Etienne, don't say that.
ETIENNE	At two bucks an hour...
VICTOR	We're in public, Etienne.
ETIENNE	With pigeons shittin' on our heads all day long...
VICTOR	That never happened.
ETIENNE	They've been shittin' on *my* head since the day you dragged me in here.
VICTOR	The pigeons didn't shit on our heads, Etienne! Don't say that, you have no right to say that. They didn't shit on our heads once. It's not true. It isn't true. And she isn't a nutcase, OK? Don't say that either. And anyway, we don't know, maybe she'll come tomorrow? Maybe tomorrow. For sure. We don't know.

Silence.

ETIENNE Let's go. We're gettin' outta here.

They don't move.

LUCE *Off* So many lives, all living things, so many lives have been snuffed out...

Blackout.

The End

Postscript:
A Farewell to Samuel Beckett

A night in December 1989

I have a passion for Samuel Beckett's work. It just took hold of me—it's not my fault, passion just happens, for better or worse, that's how it is. Today, learning of his death, I'm still hung up with this very personal play written in the spirit of Godot, for months I've crammed myself full of that pitiless anxiety and the beauty of that idleness. But if passion inspires, it also rends your heart, sometimes until it steeps the soul in sadness, a night like tonight which has become for me, through the power of memory, poetry and drink, like a kind of mourning.

I have just learned of Beckett's death and to comfort myself, I dream about the day when I was travelling in Italy—I had already been wandering for months in search of I don't know what, Ulysses without Penelope—and where, in a drunken slumber, I was robbed of everything I owned. My backpack, my books, my toothbrush, a notebook with the addresses of friends made through chance encounters while travelling, and a ridiculous red latex clown nose that I was carrying with the idea that sooner or later I would do clown performances in public squares to let the world know I was there. And so I found myself naked before the world and far away from my mother, and all the thief had left me so I could hang on to life exiled in this country where I could barely stammer out the language was my passport and Beckett's *Waiting for Godot*. In my passion I told myself that I still had the most important thing, intoxicated as I was with my own wandering. Well, enough of that.

Beckett, who said that his life will be nothing more than a stain upon the silence, is the greatest dramatic author of the end of the millennium. Perhaps the greatest author, period. Maybe the last, too. After Beckett there is nothing left to say, nothing left to reveal, to discover. The word is disembodied. All that's left is the voice, relentlessly seeking meaning; no meaning being found, the voice errs and loses its way, tirelessly meandering in search of another voice, which is also searching.

Beckett's first characters were wanderers—Ulysseses without Ithacas. Their odysseys lead them nowhere and they have trouble telling us how they got there. The characters of his last novel are still wanderers who, now lying in muck, claw at the ground in search of another, die of exhaustion and of helplessness. Like the millions of Jews, Ethiopians, Cambodians, and all those men and women found dead over the last fifty years in mass graves, these millions of bodies lying in muck, in dire straits, the final stage of this wandering of men of which Beckett was the bard, a man who was always said to be apolitical.

For the last forty years, Beckett's voice has always been with us. After the great novels and plays it was heard less and less often, but it never altogether disappeared, courageously attempting to iterate and reiterate human privation, the emptiness of existence, the grotesque tragedy of human misery, where nothing happens but horror, insignificance, misunderstanding, aging, and decay. Fortunately, with humour and tenderness, "In the beginning was the pun," he would say wryly.

Beckett had the courage of his works stamped harshly on his face. That eagle-like face, lined like a roadmap unfolded a thousand times by a traveller in search of meaning. A face hardened from his wandering to the bottom of that "air full of our cries," where "habit is a great deadener." A face bitter from having encountered the failure of human experience and from having dedicated his whole life to this failure, caught between tenderness and helplessness, and with merciless brilliance.

I salute you Mr. Beckett. Rest in peace, it's all over now. For good. And alone with your work, our faculties exhausted and our imaginations half dead, we will continue to seek the courage to live.